MaKiNG FaCeS

Toby Forward
Illustrated by James Marsh

Hamish Hamilton · London

"Miss,"
said Daisy.
"Kate's making
faces."
"Stop that, Kate,"
said Miss, but
she didn't look
up, so Kate
carried on.

She made a cat face for
Daisy, who hissed at her.
Bill licked his lips, so Kate
made a dog face for him.

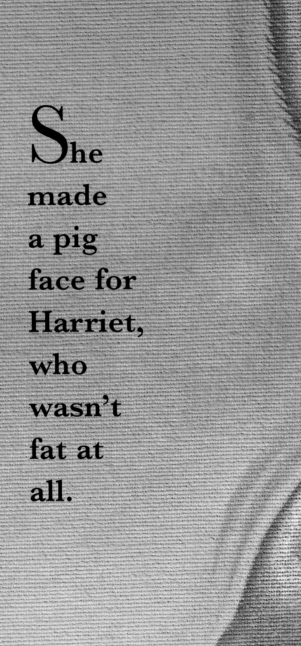

She made a pig face for Harriet, who wasn't fat at all.

And a mouse
face for Alice,
who squeaked
with delight.
Miss looked
up to see what
all the noise was
about, so Kate
made her a
curious face,
like an owl.
Miss blinked.

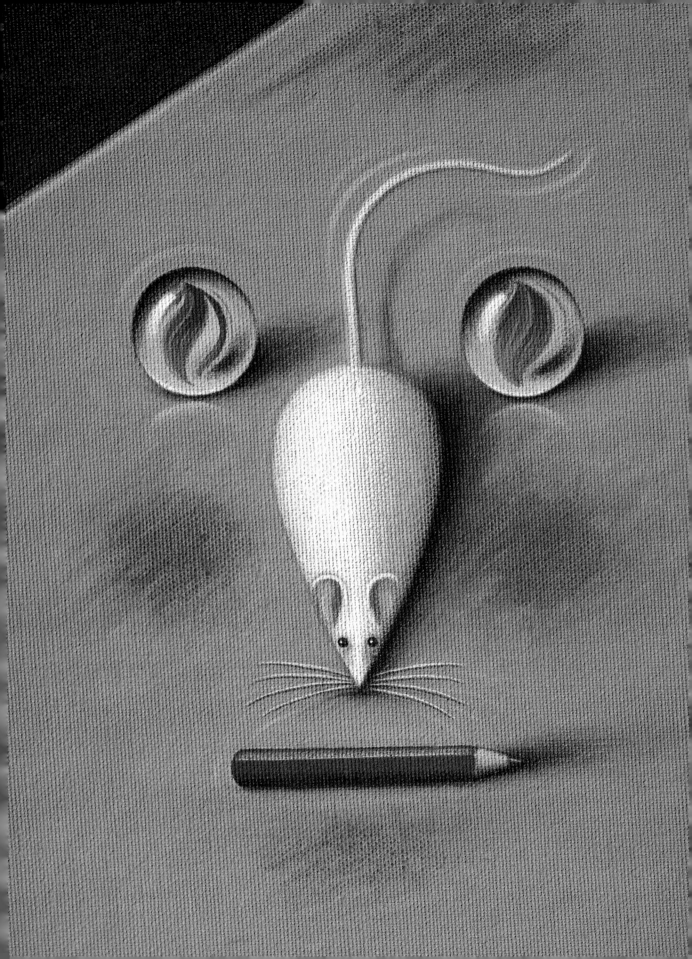

"That's wild," said Pete.
And that gave Kate an idea.
So she made a tiger's face
for him. And a fox's face
for Daniel.
And a lion's face for Jayne,
which made her look so different
that people hardly knew her.
But she liked it and said it was
just right.
And a grizzly bear.
And a hedgehog, and a rabbit.
The other children
crowded round.

"Make me a face." "Make a face for me."

So Kate made a bull, and a wild horse, and a panther. And a wolf for Lucy, who was not quite comfortable with it. Then she made herself a leopard's face, which was just right for her.
She sprang up, gave a great roar, and called them to follow her.

They all rushed
out of the classroom,
Miss fluttering above
them and hooting,
to-whit-to-whoo.

They ran through the school,
out across the playground,
into the street, and down the road.

They ran into
shops and
people screamed.
Their eyes
gleamed, and
their teeth shone.
Their claws
clicked on the
hard floor of the
supermarket,
and their breath
steamed into
freezers.

The whole
town ran from
them in terror,
and the cat and
the hedgehog
and the mouse
and the rabbit
looked round in
wonder, and
scurried quietly
along after
the others.

A police car came swerving round the corner, its siren blaring, its lights flashing.

But when the policemen saw the lion and the panther and the leopard they turned around and rushed away.

Silently the class paced their way through the deserted town, stopping sometimes to sniff in dark corners or to make a low, threatening rumble of a roar. Miss fluttered above them, trying helplessly to drive them back to school. To-whit-to-whoo. But they ignored her.

A door opened
and an old woman
looked out.
"Where is everyone?"
she asked.
"They've run away,"
said Kate. "Because
they're frightened
of us."
And she roared,
to frighten the
old woman away.
The old woman
looked at Kate and
all the other
wild animals.

She made a small noise in
her throat, and put out her hand.
The cat and the hedgehog and
the mouse and the rabbit ran
to her, and she picked them up
and cuddled them.
Kate roared again.
Then the old woman looked at
Kate and she made a face of
her own.

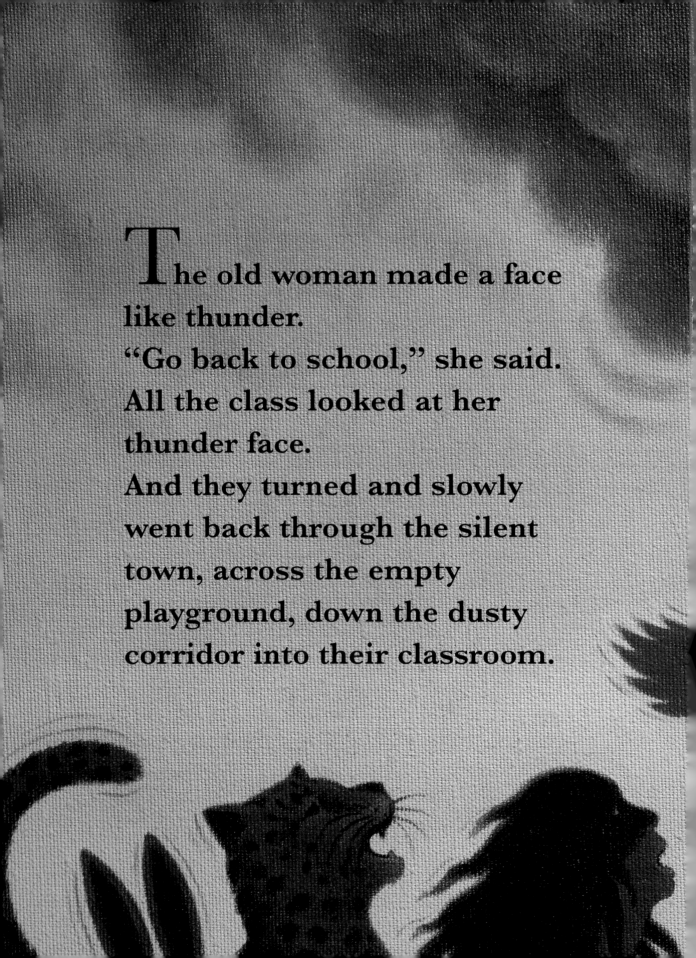

The old woman made a face
like thunder.
"Go back to school," she said.
All the class looked at her
thunder face.
And they turned and slowly
went back through the silent
town, across the empty
playground, down the dusty
corridor into their classroom.

Then they took off their
faces and put them in the bin.
Including Miss.
"That's better," she said. "Kate?"
"Yes, Miss?"
"Don't make faces again, please."
Kate nodded. "No, Miss."
But she thought to herself...
next time...